...and all the ships at sea

...and all the ships at sea

Tales told in the wardroom, chiefs quarters, and about the mess decks

A collection of short stories
by
Captain R. J. Schuster

Tri Star Book Books

***

The sources for all the stories included herein swear them to be true. In some cases the names have been changed to protect the privacy of the individuals involved.

All rights reserved. No part of this book may be reproduced without permission from the publisher.

Library of Congress Number Pending

ISBN: 978-1-88987-05-7

Copyright 2008, R. J. Schuster

Printed in USA

Tri Star Books

***

This book is dedicated to all the men and women who serve or who have served on all the ships at sea.

Other books by R. J. Schuster

An Act of Betrayal, America's Involvement in the Bay of Pigs

Rush to Armageddon, The race to build the hydrogen bomb

The Colraine Years, Life in a Southern Manor

Operation Red Dragon

Contents

Preface
The Rogue Destroyer (1)
The Mother-in-law (8)
Don't Tangle with the Wrangell (13)
A Matter of Priorities (20)
The Party (26)
Lost at Sea (29)
The Officers Club (37)
The Potato Battle (41)
A Game of Chicken (45)
The Big Boat Race (51)
The Saga of the Willie Dee (59)
The Homecoming (66)

Preface

The swapping of stories and telling yarns has been going on as long as men, and now women, have gone down to the sea in ships. In this book, I have attempted to put some of these *sea stories*, as they are commonly called, down on paper. Although I believe their contents to be true, it would be foolhardy of me to say that they have not been embellished a bit in the telling and retelling. After all, that is part of the nature of sailors.

In some cases I am sure the reader has heard some of the stories told here. If so, I apologize. I make no claim that they are original. I am also certain that each of you has stories of your own that are equally as bizarre or funny.

For the title of the book, I borrowed from the famous broadcaster of the World War II era, Walter Winchell, who opened each of his broadcasts with the sound of a telegraph key in the background, over which he said, "Good evening, Mr. and Mrs. North and South America *and all the ships at sea.*"

Chapter 1

The Rogue Destroyer

In the "tin can" Navy, seamanship and ship handling have long been considered the hallmarks of a good skipper. Accordingly, there is a great deal of competition among the various captains to show off their abilities in this area. One of the best opportunities to do that lay in bringing a ship to a landing alongside the pier. When done properly, the ship would move in smartly toward the pier and come to a stop alongside with only the minimum amount of maneuvering involved. There were times, however, when things did not go as planned. This was one of those times.

The year was 1950. The Korean War had just begun. At the Naval Base at Pearl Harbor, the ships of CORTDESRON 2, (escort destroyer squadron 21), commonly known as the Pineapple Squadron, honed their ASW (anti-submarine warfare) skills in preparation for their upcoming deployment to WESTPAC (western pacific). The squadron was made up in large part of World War II vintage Fletcher Class destroyers. They had just finished refitting in the shipyard where they had undergone an extensive conversion to DDEs. Equipped with the latest in sonar gear and anti-submarine warfare weaponry, they were the elite of the Navy's sub-hunting forces. The USS *Renshaw* was one of these destroyers. A veteran of many battles in the Pacific during World War II, she also had the distinction of being the ship President Harry Truman had ridden when he reviewed the fleet during the Victory Day celebration in New York Harbor at the end of the war.

With the advent of the Cold War, the Navy had become increasingly concerned with the growing Soviet submarine capabilities. Hence, in Navy circles there was a great deal of emphasis on developing a counter-capability to deal with this threat. As part of this effort, Navy officials in Washington decided to assign a select group of submarine officers to command these newly outfitted ships, in the belief that their knowledge of submarine tactics would help develop counter tactics to outsmart their adversaries. Commander Chuck Langstrom was one of these skippers. Although at times a little overwhelmed, he nevertheless was a quick learner and was catching on fast. Unfortunately, it would prove not to be fast enough.

One day the *Renshaw* was returning to port from a day of working with a submarine in the operating areas south of Oahu. Entering the channel, she rounded Hospital Point and passed close aboard the wreck of the USS Arizona, lying on the bottom where she had been sunk by Japanese dive bombers on December 7, 1941.

After rendering side honors to the fallen comrades entombed there, she turned ninety degrees, passed the Pearl Harbor Naval Shipyard to starboard, and approached her designated berth at the Naval Station sub base piers. The berth she was assigned lay alongside the pier between two nests of destroyers. It was a little after 1600 hours. Working hours had just ended at the sub base, and base employees hoping to avoid the rush hour traffic were hurrying to their cars in the parking lot alongside the pier.

Typical of Pearl, the weather was warm and sunny, with just a hint of the trade winds blowing. The mountains straddling the island to the north blocked the brunt of their force. The *Renshaw*'s approach was routine, and although not perfect, it was still a respectable showing. The destroyer *Nicholas,* which had been working with the *Renshaw* earlier conducting coordinated ASW attacks, was assigned to nest outboard of the *Renshaw.*

Onboard the *Renshaw,* the deck divisions were in the process of doubling up the lines. As what would have been normal practice, the skipper gave the order to secure the special sea detail except for line handlers, but for some unknown reason he decided to keep the main engines on line while they waited for the *Nicholas* to tie up alongside to seaward.

In the engine room, the chief on watch wondered why the skipper wanted to keep the engines on line. He decided to go have a look-see topside.

Meanwhile, below decks, in main engine control, the throttle man on watch requested permission from the bridge to spin main engines every three minutes. This was standard operating procedure, since failing to do so would run the risk that propeller shafts would freeze up in the shaft bearings.

On the bridge the telephone talker called out, "Main engine control requests permission to spin main engines, sir."

"Very well, permission granted," the skipper replied.

The captain was unaware that when he had given the order to secure the sea detail, the personnel on duty in the IC Room (internal communications room) had turned off the power to all gauges in the engine room.

While all this was going on, in main engine control, the throttle man, having received permission to spin main engines, cracked the throttle open. He watched the RPM counter mounted in front of him. It didn't move.

"What the hell?" he thought.

He opened the throttle a little wider. Then a little wider. Still nothing. It didn't occur to him that the power to the RPM indicator had been turned off.

By this time the screws had revved up until they approached standard speed. One has to be a destroyer man to appreciate the tremendous power of these engines and their ability to accelerate quickly.

The ship surged ahead. The lines securing the ship to the pier became taut, took on a heavy strain, and then began to part. The crack of the lines breaking caused everyone on the pier to stop. They wondered what was going on. To their amazement, what they saw was the *Renshaw* take off and barrel down the pier like some sort of wild beast.

On board the *Nicholas*, the skipper let out a loud "What the devil is going on here?" before giving the order for all engines to back full, but not before dealing the *Renshaw* a glancing blow.

By now the *Renshaw*, free of all lines, had built up a full head of steam and was heading directly for the sterns of the two destroyers nested up ahead.

Two seamen on a punt, tied up alongside the stern of the inboard destroyer, were touching up paint. Hearing the commotion going on behind them, they turned around to have a look. What they saw gave them good reason to panic. The bow of a destroyer was bearing down on them, at what appeared to be full speed. Frightened out of their wits, they followed their instincts. One jumped into the water and paddled frantically for the pier, hoping to seek safety under it. The other scrambled up the line securing the punt to the fantail, all the while screaming at the top of his lungs for help.

By now the in-port watch on the quarterdeck of the destroyers nested in front of the *Renshaw* saw what was happening and realized their peril. Desperately they sounded the collision alarm.

On the pier, people stood aghast, looking on helplessly. Onboard the *Renshaw*, line handlers frantically tried to get a line, any line, onto the pier.

Finally, luck broke in favor of the wayward destroyer. Either the sequence of the lines parting, or the glancing blow from the *Nicholas* caused the *Renshaw* to miss the sterns of both the destroyers nested ahead. Instead, she deftly passed between them, neatly cutting the lines of the outboard destroyer in the nest, setting her adrift in the stream.

Needless to say, on the bridge of the *Renshaw* everything was in pandemonium as the bridge team frantically attempted to find out what was going on. The only thing that was apparent was that they were barreling down the pier out of control.

Watching the sterns of the destroyers tied up ahead loom ever larger, the skipper pushed down the button on the 21MC and shouted into the speaker, "All engines back full. *All engines back full."*

About the same time the captain was screaming into the 21MC, the chief on watch in the engine room realized something was very wrong. Scurrying down the ladder, he quickly assessed the situation. Pushing the throttle man aside, he grabbed the wheel and spun it shut. At the same time he heard the captain's voice on the 21MC frantically calling for "all back full." Quickly he shifted the engines into reverse and spun the throttle wide open.

With engines in reverse, the twin screws bit into the water, bringing the destroyer to a stop a few feet from ramming the head of the pier.

Disaster had been averted for the moment. But before the onlookers on the pier could breathe a sigh of relief, they were confronted with a new set of circumstances. Instead of charging down the pier, the rogue destroyer was now backing down the pier in full reverse. It was now time for the two destroyers nested astern to sound their collision alarms. All the while this was going on, the line handlers on the ship desperately tried to get a line secured to the pier. Each time they succeeded, the line quickly parted.

"All engines stop. **All engines stop**," the captain screamed into the 21MC.

In the engine room the chief spun the throttle closed. At long last the unruly beast slowed down enough so that the line handlers could get the remnants of the mooring lines around the bollards on the pier. Finally the ship came to a stop.

By now a tugboat had arrived on the scene and managed to get the destroyer that was set adrift safely tied up alongside the destroyer ahead. Onlookers on the pier got into their cars and drove off, no doubt to relay the account of the events they had just witnessed to their wives over dinner.

It would be a long time before the ship's company could show up in any of the various clubs on the base or bars in town without being greeted by a chorus of "Whoop, whoop," mimicking the sound of a ship's collision alarm.

Chapter 2

The Mother-in-law

Onboard a destroyer tied up at Pearl Harbor, a group of officers sat around the wardroom table. They passed away the time, as sailors are inclined to do everywhere, drinking coffee and swapping sea stories. During a lull in the conversation, one of them looked across the table in the direction of the staff chaplain, saying, "Padre, I'll bet you've come across some strange tales in your time. Would you care to share any of them with us?"

Chaplain Murphy paused for a moment. A slight smile crossed his face. "As a matter of fact, there is one story that comes to mind," he replied. "It happened while I was the base chaplain right here in Pearl."

"One day I was in my office working on my homily for the Sunday service when there was a knock on the door. It was my assistant. He said there was a seaman outside in the reception area who wished to talk to me.

"Any idea what he wants to see me about?" I asked.

"No, sir. He wouldn't say," the yeoman replied.

"Okay, send him in," I said.

A few seconds later a young man appeared in the doorway. He was obviously very nervous. Seeking to put him at ease, I motioned toward a couch off to the side of my desk.

"Have a seat," I said.

He sat down. After he was seated, I continued, "My yeoman said you wanted to see me. What is it I can do for you?"

The young sailor hesitated. Then he began to speak. "Padre, I have a real problem. I don't know quite where to start."

"Why not start at the beginning?" I said.

He paused briefly, as if to get his thoughts in order, then he began to tell his story. He was hesitant at first, but after a few moments he began to relax a little. It was like he was glad to get off his chest what he was about to tell me.

"Well, you see, sir, it started about a year and a half ago. I was assigned to duty at the Naval Shipyard in Boston. Except for boot camp, it was the first time I had ever really been away from home. I was lonely.

"One weekend I went to a dance sponsored by the USO. While there I met a local girl. We hit it off pretty good, and when the evening was over I asked her out on a date. It wasn't long before we became serious, and several months later I asked her to marry me. We set a date for the wedding. It was to be in June, after she graduated from high school.

"Unfortunately, in March I got a set of orders to the Naval Station at Pearl Harbor. That evening I broke the news to my fiancée and her mother. I told them the wedding would have to be postponed.

"My girlfriend broke down in tears. Her mother was beside herself. I later found out that earlier, when she was a young girl, the mother's own boyfriend had run off, leaving her pregnant." His voice trailed off.

"Well, what happened?" I asked. My interest was now piqued.

"My future mother-in-law suggested we push up the wedding date. I told her it was okay with me, but my girlfriend said she wouldn't agree to getting married unless her mother could go along with us to my new duty station.

"I didn't have a problem with that. The problem was that while I knew the Navy would pay for my wife's transportation, I wasn't so sure about my mother-in-law. On a seaman's pay I knew I sure couldn't afford it, but I agreed to check into it.

"The next day I stopped by the personnel office. They confirmed what I thought to be true. They would pay a wife's transportation, but not that of a mother-in-law.

"That evening I went back over to their house and gave them the bad news.

"I guess we'll just have to postpone the wedding until I can save up some money," I said. With that my fiancée broke down in tears.

"Wait a minute," my future mother-in-law said. Maybe we can come up with something. I have an idea. Maybe this will work. You said the Navy would pay for your wife's transportation, didn't you?"

"Yes, that's right," I replied.

"How about dependents?" she asked.

"I'm not sure, but I guess they would," I replied. "But how would that affect us. I don't have any dependents."

"What if you were to marry *me*?" she said. "That way, Sheryl would become your dependent."

I don't know," I said. This seemed a bit bizarre. I looked over at Sheryl to see her reaction.

"It'll only be on paper," she said. "After we get to Hawaii you and Mom could get a divorce and then we could get married."

"I still don't know," I replied. "This is weird."

"You don't want to marry me," my girlfriend said, again breaking into tears.

"That's the point. I do want to marry you," I replied. "I just don't want to marry your mother."

"It would only be for a short time," her mother said.

"Although I still wasn't sure, in the end I agreed to the arrangement."

He paused for a moment. I took the opportunity to interrupt. "I can't say that I approve of the arrangement, but I'm curious. Did you go through with the marriage?"

"Oh, yes, sir,' the young sailor replied. "In fact, we are all living together in Navy housing."

"I presume you are here then to ask me about getting a divorce or an annulment," I said.

"Oh, no, sir," the young man replied.

I was perplexed. "What then?" I asked.

He lowered his head. "Well, you see, sir, both of them are pregnant."

Chapter 3

Don't Tangle with the Wrangell

Probably one of the worst duty assignments in the Navy, if not the worst, is being assigned to an ammunition ship. Not only is the work backbreaking, the cargo dangerous, but even when you did get in to port for liberty, your ship would be treated like a pariah, assigned a berth in an explosive anchorage, as far away as possible from the fleet landing. It was widely rumored that detailers and assignment desks at EPDOLANT (enlisted personnel distribution office Atlantic fleet) reserved these assignments for someone with whom they wanted to get even.

The *Wrangell* was an ammunition ship assigned to the Sixth Fleet in the Mediterranean. Her new skipper was Captain Edward Bingham. What he had done to get on the wrong side of his detailer is not known.

What we do know is that he was different from his peers. Early in his career, instead of choosing to become a traditional fixed-wing aviator, he decided to become a free-flight balloon pilot. It was widely rumored that the lack of oxygen at high altitudes had affected his behavior. It wasn't that he was not a competent seaman. In fact, the reverse was true. It was just that he chose to do things in a somewhat non-traditional way.

When he took command of the *Wrangell*, morale was at a low ebb. The crew grumbled over the hard work, lack of appreciation, and particularly their being treated like the plague when they entered port. If by chance the weather was too bad to run liberty boats, they often didn't even get to go ashore on liberty.

Captain Bingham realized that there was little he could do about the work or where they were berthed in port. If he was going to improve the morale of his crew, he had to think of something else.

The first thing he did was to come up with a ship's motto. He decided on *"Don't tangle with the Wrangell."* He had signs made up and posted all around the ship. Slowly it caught on with the crew, and soon after that it started appearing on hats and jackets. The radiomen even began to include it at the end of all outgoing radio messages.

Next, Bingham set up a school onboard and proclaimed himself the dean of the College of Nautical Knowledge. Classes were held in English, mathematics and any other subject in which the crew expressed an interest and where an instructor could be found to teach the course. Graduation ceremonies were held frequently, with the captain substituting a mortarboard for his gold-braided captain's cap to hand out diplomas.

Morale began to improve. The sailors began to adopt that special swagger often attributed to sailors everywhere. While all this was fine, the one thing that grabbed the crew's attention more than anything else was the antics of the skipper himself. He took every opportunity to inject a little humor into the daily shipboard activities no matter how outrageous it might be.

One of his more famous pranks occurred when the ship was in port in Barcelona, Spain. For a change the ship was berthed alongside a pier. Someone ashore must have screwed up.

In any event, one evening the skipper was returning to the ship late when he noticed a vendor with a donkey near the head of the pier. Waving a twenty-dollar bill in front of him, Captain Bingham asked if he could borrow the man's donkey for a little while. He promised to return the animal unharmed. The old man jumped at the opportunity. Hell, he would have *sold* him the donkey for twenty bucks.

Leading the beast by a rope, the skipper approached the ship's gangway. He called out to the quarterdeck above, asking for help in getting the donkey up the gangway. The donkey wasn't very sure about going up the narrow gangway, but with a little encouragement and a lot of shoving from the rear they somehow managed to get the animal onto the quarterdeck.

"Okay, take this animal down to the chief's quarters," Bingham ordered. "When you get him there, tie him up and report back to me."

It was after taps, and most everyone had already turned in.

If getting the donkey up the gangway was difficult, it was even harder to get him down the ladder and into the chief's quarters. However, it was captain's orders, so after a good deal of struggle they finally managed to get the donkey down below and tied it up in the chiefs mess as the skipper had requested. When they were done they reported back to the captain, who was waiting on the quarterdeck.

Hearing the news, Bingham then ordered the boatswain's mate to pipe the word over the public address system for all chief's to get their ass on the quarterdeck on the double.

Jarred awake by the sound of the 1MC, there were a few "*What the hells!*" and some other oaths that can't be repeated here. When they saw the donkey they realized what was going on. *The captain was just up to another one of his pranks.*

On another occasion, during a scheduled replenishment at sea, the captain sent out a message to the carrier *Essex* that he intended to transfer the "thing" to them while they were alongside. He also made the commander of the Sixth Fleet and all other ships in the fleet as information addressees on the message.

Onboard the *Essex,* the skipper wondered what was going on, but, not wishing to let on that he didn't know, he decided to take a wait-and-see attitude.

As the *Essex* made her approach to go alongside the *Wrangell,* the skipper noticed a large container covered with canvass sitting on the deck of the *Wrangell,* obviously waiting to be transferred over by hi-line. He concluded that this must be the "thing" referred to in the message. Suddenly it became clear. The message was referring to a nuclear weapon. He called for the special weapons officer and ordered him to send a handling team to the forward elevator in preparation for receiving special weapons.

When the hi-line was secured, the "thing" was carefully hooked on and made its slow passage across the open water separating the two ships. Upon its arrival, the shrouded container was carefully lowered to the deck of the carrier. After it was unhooked, the special weapons team moved in to take custody. They slowly removed the cover, only to discover, not a nuclear bomb, but a replica of a two-holer outhouse.

Watching the events unfold from the bridge of the *Wrangell,* Bingham called out for the radio messenger. He handed him a message. "Get this out as soon as you can," he directed. The message was addressed to COMSIXFLT. It read as follows: *The thing successfully transferred to Essex while alongside.*

When he received the message, Admiral Brown, on his flagship, wondered what was going on. He remembered reading the previous message from the *Wrangell.* He decided it was time to get to the bottom of this. He directed his aide to get the skipper of the *Essex* on the horn.

A couple of seconds later the aide reported, "The captain of the *Essex* is standing by on the radio, sir."

By now all the ships in the task force were listening in. They were as curious as the admiral was.

Picking up the handset, Admiral Brown said, "Snuffy, can you tell me what the hell is going on? What is this goddamn 'thing' I am hearing about?"

The skipper then had to relay to the admiral that the "thing" was in fact a two-holer outhouse.

For once the admiral, was at a loss for words. He sputtered a little and then meekly said, "Roger, out."

Listening in on the pritac radio, Captain Bingham then ordered another message sent out addressed to all ships in the Sixth Fleet. All it said was "Don't tangle with the *Wrangell*."

Chapter 4

A Matter of Priorities

Serving on a minesweeper was one of the more hazardous duties during the Korean War. During the course of the war, the North Koreans had acquired a large number of mines from both their Chinese and Russian allies. Cheap and effective, they provided a means to deny United Nations forces the use of North Korean harbors and inlets. There was also the possibility that the enemy would get lucky and sink or severely damage a major warship. It remained the duty of the lowly minesweeper to do the nasty and dirty job of sweeping and destroying as many of these lethal weapons as possible. Still, in spite of their heroic efforts, the Navy continued to lose an average of one ship a month from inadvertently striking a mine.

Along the northeast coast of the Korean peninsula, Lieutenant Commander Dusty Rhodes was the commanding officer of one of the sweeps assigned to keep the coastal waters clear of mines. It proved to be exasperating duty. It seemed that as fast as he cleared an area, the North Koreans would re-sow it with mines, sometimes in a matter of days.

When it was his turn to speak during the weekly commanding officers conferences onboard the carrier *Bon Homme Richard,* Rhodes continually pleaded for air strikes on suspected mine storage depots. Being only a lieutenant commander, however, his requests continued to fall on deaf ears. He was constantly reminded that there were other higher priority targets out there, and besides, he didn't have any real proof as to where the depots were located anyway. Having to deal with his requests being repeatedly turned down week after week, Rhodes became increasingly frustrated. He determined that he would show them. If they wanted proof, by God, he would get them proof.

The following week, after he had finished sweeping the waters in the vicinity of Sonjin for the umpteenth time, he headed his boat toward a small village just to the south of an area where he had seen unusual activity amidst the local fishing fleet. He had long suspected that the North Korean fishing boats were actively sowing mines in his area. If that were true, he concluded, there must be a mine storage depot nearby.

Entering the small harbor, he pulled his boat up alongside a ramshackle old pier and tied up. Being far behind the front lines, the area was guarded by a local home guard made up mostly of old men and young boys.

Seeing the American vessel enter the harbor, they feared the worst and headed for the hills, leaving one frightened old man to confront the Americans. Through an interpreter, Rhodes demanded to know where the mine depot was located. Scared out of his wits, the old man volunteered to show them where the depot was. Piling into a dilapidated old vehicle, Rhodes, the old man and two armed gunner's mates headed off.

As they neared the crest of a hill, overlooking a small fishing village, the old man motioned for them to stop. Getting out, the foursome proceeded cautiously on foot. Through the brush, the old man pointed to a large frame building at the head of a pier. There appeared to be an unusual amount of activity going on. Lifting his binoculars, Rhodes confirmed what he suspected. Several carts alongside the building were laden with what appeared to be mines. He quickly snapped a number of photos with a telephoto lens, using his personal 35mm camera. Having gotten what they came for, the group beat a hasty retreat and headed back to their boat, where the rest of the crew anxiously awaited. Handing the old man a couple of packs of cigarettes, Rhodes boarded the sweep and gave the order to cast off.

At the next CO's conference, Dusty patiently waited for his turn to speak. Finally the time arrived.

"Commander Rhodes, do you have anything for us today?" the admiral said. He expected the same old request for an air strike on some suspected mine depot as in the past.

Dusty slowly got to his feet.

"Sir, I again urgently request an air strike on a mine depot located here on this chart."

From those seated around the table there was an audible groan as if to say, "Here we go again."

"How do you know this is a mine depot?" the admiral asked.

This was the moment Dusty had been waiting for. Reaching into a large manila envelope, he removed a series of photographs he had had developed and blown up in the carrier's darkroom earlier in the day.

"Sir, I have photographs of mines being loaded onto carts at the location." By now he had the attention of all the other skippers gathered around the table. They looked at him questioningly as if to ask, *"How in hell did you get those pictures?"*

"Let's have a look at what you have," the admiral directed.

Dusty passed the photos up the table. Each person handling them tried to get a glimpse before passing them along. When they got to the admiral, he carefully looked them over. He then passed them on to the skipper of the *Bon Homme Richard.* "What do you think, Joe?" he asked. Captain Joe Hoskins studied them carefully. Passing the photos to the air boss, he said, "They look authentic to me." Pausing for a second, he continued, "If you don't mind my asking, Captain, how in hell did you get these photos?

"I took them myself," Dusty replied. He didn't elaborate any further.

The admiral raised his eyebrows. "You took them yourself?" he said.

"Yes, sir, I did," Dusty replied. "It seemed like it was the only way I was going to get an air strike approved."

"Okay, I won't press you for details," the admiral replied. "You've made your point, captain." Directing his attention to the skipper of the *Bon Homme Richard* he said, "See that the captain here gets his air strike."

On the way out of the wardroom, after the conference had ended, one of Dusty's classmates at the Naval Academy came over to him. Putting his arm around his shoulder, he said, "You wouldn't want to tell your old buddy here how you managed to get those pictures, would you?"

"As I said, I took them myself," Dusty replied. "Maybe I'll fill you in on the details someday at the club in Yokosuka. That is, if you're buying," he added.

The following day Dusty received a message from the commander of the task force reporting that an air strike had been conducted that morning, and the mine depot had been destroyed.

Chapter 5

The Party

Lieutenant Colonel Nick Jensen was a tough, hard bitten, kick-ass, Marine. He lived and breathed the Corps. The words "Semper fi" were not just a motto. They were the code by which he lived. He truly believed that his Marines were the toughest, meanest group of fighting men that had ever inhabited the Earth. As an infantry battalion commander, he constantly reminded his officers and men of this fact and the standards they were expected to live up to.

While on deployment in Okinawa, his battalion had just completed a joint training exercise in conjunction with their Japanese counterparts. To celebrate this event, Jensen invited the Japanese marine officers to a party at the "O" club.

In keeping with their image, the battalion used an old commode that they had rescued from the scrap yard for the battalion punchbowl. In anticipation of their guest arrival, the punchbowl had been filled with a concoction of various types of alcohol and other ingredients so that the contents resembled what the contents of a recently used commode should look like. For added realism, the "gunny" had tossed in a few Clark chocolate bars.

By the time their guests arrived the party was already well under way. Jensen greeted his guests at the door.

"Welcome," he said, shouting above the din of the celebrants in the room behind him. "Come on in. Join the party. How about a little libation to get things started?"

With that, he escorted the Japanese marines to the center of the room where the punchbowl sat prominently on a table. Calling for everyone's attention, he said, "Listen up everybody."

The room became quiet as all eyes focused on the host.

"I would like to propose a toast to our guests, Jensen said, picking up a tin cup sitting on the table and dipping it in to the commode. He motioned for the Japanese commander to follow suit.

Hesitantly the Japanese officer picked up a cup and dipped it in to the commode. He tried not to look at the contents of the bowl. By now, all he hoped for was that he wasn't going to get sick in front of everyone.

After his guest had filled his cup, Jensen raised his cup in toast. "To our Japanese friends, stalwart marines all, and almost as good as United States Marines." He downed the contents of his cup in one gulp and looked over at his Japanese counterpart, obviously waiting for him to follow suit. The Japanese officer was by now thoroughly intimidated. He realized, however, that there was no turning back. Slowly raising his cup, he closed his eyes and downed the contents of his cup.

Jensen had had his fun. Not wishing to embarrass his guest any further, he proclaimed, "Let the party begin." With that he dipped his cup back in to the commode and refilled it.

The Japanese marines had by now regained their composure and joined in. As the evening progressed, one of them even went so far as to reach his hand into the bowl to retrieve one of the chocolate bars. He bit into it, professing to all that he was hungry.

Chapter 6

Lost at Sea

James H. Billings III graduated from Dartmouth College on June 6, 1945 summa cum laude. On that date he also received a commission as an ensign, U.S. Navy. World War II was nearing an end, and while most everyone was looking forward to getting out and retuning home, Ensign Billings' career was only just beginning. A true heads-and-shoulders type, he had graduated well ahead of the majority of his classmates in class standing. He looked forward to beginning his new career, and aspired to be the youngest admiral in the U.S. Navy.

With his sheepskin and a packet containing his orders in hand, he went back to his dorm room, where he eagerly opened the envelope. He couldn't believe it. He had been assigned to command of an LCI based on Guam. He had hoped for a destroyer assignment, but to get a shot at command the first time out was more than he could have ever hoped for.

Taking a few weeks of leave, he said goodbye to friends and family, packed his sea bag, and boarded a train in Boston for the long cross-country trip to San Francisco. Arriving there in early August, he checked in with the travel office for onward travel to Guam. He was told that there was an MSTS transport leaving the following Tuesday for Guam and points west, with a stopover in Hawaii. He eagerly looked forward to the stopover in Hawaii.

Checking into the BOQ (Bachelor Officer Quarters) at the Naval Station Treasure Island, he unpacked his bags. He had three days in which to enjoy the sights in San Francisco before boarding the transport. With the war over in Europe and the war in the Pacific ending, San Francisco was filled with sailors. The bars were overflowing, and young Billings joined in on the fun.

On Tuesday morning, he repacked his gear and called for a base taxi to take him into the city. There he boarded the *USNS General Sherman* and checked into his assigned stateroom. He looked forward to getting to sea. After all, this was what sailors did for a living. Nine days later the Sherman pulled into Pearl Harbor to drop off passengers before continuing on to Guam.

Billings had by now gotten his sea legs, and was beginning to feel like an honest-to-goodness sailor.

Arriving at Apra Harbor in Guam, Billings called for base transportation. He anxiously awaited the first look at his new command. When she came into sight he was a bit disappointed. She was not the sleek greyhound of the sea he had conjured up in his mind. Instead, there was a rusting, squared-off, somewhat oversized landing craft not even as big as an LST. He quickly put his misgivings aside. This was his ship....his first command.

Walking up the gangway, he turned and faced the stern and saluted smartly before stepping on to the quarterdeck. Addressing the petty officer on watch, he said, "Ensign Billings reporting for duty."

Returning the salute, the petty officer replied, "Welcome aboard, sir." Turning to the messenger of the watch he directed, "Messenger, escort Ensign Billings to the captain's cabin."

"Follow me, sir," the messenger said.

Arriving outside the captain's stateroom, the messenger knocked on the door. "Captain, Ensign Billings is here, sir."

"Send him in."

Inside, Lt.(jg) Fitzpatrick was in his skivvies. He stood up and held out his hand, "You don't know how glad I am to see you. Welcome to the gator navy," he said somewhat sarcastically. "Pardon the dress, but it is so damned hot here."

Billings wasn't sure what to make of it. His midshipman training hadn't quite prepared him for this.

By way of conversation, he asked, "What's your next duty station?"

"Next duty station?" Fitzpatrick exclaimed. "Hell, I'm a reserve. Now that the war is over, I'm outta here. Don't care if I ever see a ship again."

After a brief turnover process, Billings assumed command. His euphoria somewhat diminished, he faced up to the challenge. Now with the war over, most everyone onboard anxiously awaited his separation orders. Faced with an ever-diminishing crew, the new CO worried about if and when any replacements would be arriving. So far they had not been asked to put to sea, but had spent their time languishing in port.

After a few weeks Billings began to adjust to the informal life style of the gator navy. He was beginning to enjoy his role as commanding officer. But things were about to change.

One morning, as he was on his second cup of coffee, the radio messenger knocked on the door to his tiny combination office and sleeping quarters.

"OP Immediate from COMPHIBPAC (commander amphibious forces Pacific), captain."

Taking the message board from him, Billings read through it. It read as follows:

FROM: COMPHIBPAC
ACTION: USS LCI 820
INFO: NAVBASE GUAM/ CINCPAC/ COMNAVFE
PROCEED TO NAVAL STATION JINGZHOU CHINA. UPON ARRIVAL CHOP [CHANGE

OPERATION CONTROL] TO COMNAVFE [COMMANDER NAVAL FORCES FAR EAST] AND AWAIT FURTHER ORDERS BT
FILE MOVREP [MOVEMENT REPORT] BT

Initialing the message he handed the board back to the messenger, saying, "Have the petty officer of the watch give me a call."

A few moments later the phone rang. "Chief Bohansky here, sir."

"Cancel all liberty, Chief. We just received orders to put to sea. "Pass the word for all departments to make ready to go to sea. Also, have the quartermaster bring charts of the western Pacific up to my cabin."

After he hung up the phone, it suddenly occurred to him that the first class quartermaster had been detached a couple of weeks ago, and his replacement had not yet arrived. The only other person in the navigation department was a quartermaster seaman striker. That meant the responsibility for navigation would rest entirely on Billings' shoulders. The thought of navigating a ship across eighteen hundred miles of open water made him uneasy, to say the least. Although he had taken a course in navigation as part of his NROTC training, it had been over a year ago. He also remembered that on the day they were scheduled to practice using a sextant, it had been cloudy. The stark reality was; *that he had absolutely no experience in actually taking a celestial sight.*

He did know how to draw a rhumb line course, however, and when the quartermaster brought the charts, he laid out a course from Guam to Jingzhou.

Two days later the LCI took in her lines from the pier at Apra and made her way out of the harbor. Once clear of the channel, Billings ordered a course set for Jingzhou. He was well aware that a DR (dead reckoning) course over such a long distance would be highly unreliable without being constantly updated by use of celestial sights. He couldn't let the crew know that he had never taken a star sight, so each morning and evening he would break out the sextant and, with his striker jotting down the readings, he would attempt to shoot the stars. He would then take the readings down to the chart room and try to reduce the sightings into LOPs (lines of position). No matter how hard he tried, he was not able to get the LOPs to cross. Without their crossing, it meant he did not have a fix of his position. Trying not to alarm the crew, he would then pretend that he had been successful in obtaining a fix, and make a mark on the chart.

The days passed. The tiny ship headed ever westward across the vast open stretch of Pacific Ocean. Each morning and evening Billings would go through his routine of pretending to take navigational sights, and making a mark on the chart. He figured that sooner or later they would make landfall in China, and after that, he reasoned, he could sail up or down the coast until he found the entrance to the bay leading to the port of Jingzhou.

Early one morning several days later, Billings was in the chart room struggling to make sense of his morning readings when the port lookout shouted out, "Land ho."

"Where away?" the OOD (Officer of the Deck) replied.

"Two points off the port bow," the lookout answered.

Hearing the exchange, Billings rushed to the bridge. He breathed a sigh of relief. They had finally made it. Now all he had to do was find out where on the China coast they were.

As the land got closer, he scanned the shoreline for sight of an inlet or harbor. Up ahead he noticed a number of small craft. He surmised them to be fishing boats returning to port after a night of fishing. He decided to follow them in. As they rounded a bend in the channel, a small village came into view. Alongside the town pier he noticed an empty spot, and decided to tie up temporarily and ask directions.

While they made fast to the pier, the young skipper noticed what looked to be a welcoming delegation coming down the pier. He made his way down to the gangway, and stepped onto the pier to greet his guests.

As they got closer he noticed that none of the faces looked Oriental. *What the hell is going on?* he thought. When they were about twenty feet away, the group stopped and one of the members, who Billings judged might be the mayor, stepped forward to greet him. Extending his hand, he said, "Welcome, American friends, to the island of Luzon. We hope you will enjoy your stay with us."

It was then that it dawned on Billings. *They weren't in China after all. Instead, they were in the Philippines.* Flustered, he shook the mayor's hand. He paused. He couldn't admit he had made an error in navigation. Besides, he reasoned, it would be impolite to reject the mayor's hospitality. "We are most pleased to be here, Mr. Mayor, and we accept your generous offer to visit your beautiful village."

For the next two days the crew enjoyed the hospitality of their newly made Filipino friends. Then the *LCI 820* got under way, rounded the northern tip of Luzon, and crossed the South China Sea to the port of Jingzhou.

Chapter 7

The Officer's Club

In 1907, to commemorate the three hundredth anniversary of the landing of the first settlers at Jamestown, the states that had been the thirteen original colonies each built a large house on the naval base at Norfolk, Virginia. Originally, these houses were used to display items relating to the early history of each of these colonies.

Once the celebration was over, these structures were turned over to the Navy Department. They still stand today, and many are still in use as living quarters for senior admirals assigned to billets in the area. One of the largest, Pennsylvania House, served as the commissioned officers club until recent years. Some of the others were converted to billeting for transient senior and junior officers.

Newly commissioned Ensign Will Johnson had just completed officer candidate training in Newport,

Rhode Island. Opening his orders, he was pleased to see that he had been assigned to a destroyer operating as part of the Sixth Fleet in the Mediterranean Gathering up his gear, he caught a hop to Norfolk aboard a flight out of Quonset Point.

Arriving at Naval Air Station Norfolk he called for a base taxi to take him to the BOQ where he checked in while awaiting onward transportation to Naples Italy where his ship was currently located.

With nothing to do while he was waiting, Johnson decided to go over to the officers club for a drink before dinner. He asked the sailor on duty at the front desk for directions.

"It's only a short distance from here. You can walk," the petty officer said. "It's the large brick building along Admiral's Row. You can't miss it."

As he walked along, Johnson came to a large, imposing brick structure. He assumed this was the club. He made his way up the walk to the front door and went inside. What he was unaware of at the time was that this was not the Officers club. Instead, it was the personal living quarters for the Commander-in-Chief Atlantic Fleet, Admiral Duncan. The officers club was actually in the building next door.

Inside the large foyer, Johnson took a look around and then went into the study off to the left side of the foyer. Taking a seat on a leather sofa beside the fireplace, he picked up a magazine from the coffee table and began to leaf through it. Admiral Duncan was seated in a leather chair on the opposite side of the room, reading the evening newspaper. Looking on in some amusement, he decided to play along.

A few moments later Duncan's steward came in to bring the admiral a drink. He looked quizzically at the young ensign sitting beside the fireplace and then over at the admiral. The admiral nodded, looked over toward the ensign, and winked at the steward. The steward guessed what had happened and went over to the Johnson. "Can I get you something to drink, sir," he said.

"I'll have a gin and tonic," Johnson replied.

The steward disappeared, returning a few moments later with the drink on a tray. He sat it down on the coffee table in front of the wayward ensign.

"Enjoy your drink, sir," he said and turned to leave the room.

Johnson sipped his drink while he continued to browse through the magazine.

About twenty minutes later the steward returned. "Could I get you another one, sir?"

"No, thanks. Just bring me the check," Johnson replied.

"The gentleman seated over there has taken care of it," the steward replied, motioning toward the admiral seated across the room.

The steward lingered in the doorway to watch.

Standing up to leave, Johnson walked over to where the admiral was seated. "I want to thank you, sir, for the drink," he said.

"It was my pleasure. I hope it was satisfactory," the admiral replied.

"Oh, the drink was fine, sir. I was expecting a little more action, though. This club is sure dead."

"It does get to be that way at this time of day," Duncan replied. "You might want to come back a little later."

Exiting the house, Johnson decided to walk down the street a little before returning to the BOQ. It was still a little while until dinner. Coming to the building next door, he saw a sign out front. It read, "Pennsylvania House, Commissioned Officers Open Mess."

How could that be? Johnson asked himself. *I just came from the Officers Club.*

Then it started to dawn on him. He walked back up the street and saw the brass plaque on the side of the house.

He couldn't believe what had happened. The commander-in-chief of the Atlantic Fleet had just bought him a drink.

Chapter 8

The Potato Battle

As with most things, certain models or designs are destined to become classics. The Ford Mustang and the 1957 Chevrolet are familiar examples that fit into this category.

In the world of ships, certain designs are classics as well. Ask any tin can sailor to name the finest class of destroyer ever built, and more than likely the answer will be "The 2100-ton Fletcher Class." Sleek, fast, and deadly, they were truly greyhounds of the sea. Whether it involved action against other ships and submarines, shore bombardment, or shooting down enemy aircraft, these ships proved their versatility and effectiveness, time and again, often against vastly superior forces. The *USS O'Bannon (DD-450)* was one of those ships.

A veteran of the war in the Pacific, her exploits are well documented in the annals of naval history. One incident, however, has to go down as one of her more unusual encounters. The story revolves around a chance encounter with a Japanese submarine, when the ship's crew members demonstrated their ingenuity to sink an enemy submarine using, of all things, potatoes.

The story has often been told wherever tin can sailors gathered around the wardroom table, in the chief's quarters, or about the mess decks. As is true with all sea stories, the specifics vary depending on who is doing the telling. Although the official action report makes no mention of the use of potatoes, the story has persisted until it has now become a part of Navy folklore. I will attempt to tell the story using the version that was related to me when I was onboard the *O'Bannon,* and what also seems to be the most logical one.

As the story goes, the *O'Bannon,* operating as part of DESRON 21, was returning from a night patrol in the Kula Gulf when she picked up a blip on her radar screen at a range of about 7000 yards. Reporting the contact to the squadron commander, she broke formation and proceeded to investigate. As she closed the range, the contact suddenly disappeared from the radar, immediately causing the skipper to suspect that the contact was a submarine. His suspicions were confirmed a short time later when sonar picked up a submerged contact dead ahead.

We caught this one napping, the skipper muttered to himself as he issued orders to stand by to roll a pattern of depth charges. As the destroyer passed over the last known position of the submarine, the pattern of depth charges detonated. The concussion waves of the charges going off reverberated throughout the hull of the ship.

Losing contact as she passed over the sub, the *O'Bannon* quickly reversed course and set up for a second run. Unfortunately, sonar was unable to regain contact with the sub. Either they had sunk the sub or she had escaped in the turbulence caused by the depth charges detonating. As per standard operating procedure, the *O'Bannon* lingered over the target, knowing that sooner or later, if the sub had survived the depth charge attack, she would eventually have to come to the surface for air and to recharge her batteries.

The hours passed slowly by without incident. Dawn came and went. Still nothing. On the wing of the bridge, the skipper dozed off in his chair.

Suddenly a noise close aboard to starboard jarred him awake. Jumping out of his chair, he rushed over to see what was going on. He was astonished to see a Japanese submarine surfacing close aboard. As the hatch opened, the sub crew rushed up on deck, firing their weapons at the destroyer.

"Commence firing," the skipper ordered excitedly. Unfortunately, the sub was too close to bring the 5-inch guns to bear. Peppered with small-arms fire, crew members took cover wherever they could. A small group huddled in the athwart ship's passageway just aft of the superstructure near to where the spud locker was located.

Unable to bring his guns to bear, the captain gave the order to fire the starboard K-guns mounted on the main deck amidships. The problem was getting to the K-guns, as the ship continued to be peppered by small arms fire. Frustrated by the turn of events, one of the sailors broke into the spud locker and began passing out potatoes to his shipmates huddled nearby. On signal, they stood up and hurled the potatoes at the sub.

The Japanese sailors, probably thinking they were hand grenades, stopped firing and took cover. Taking advantage of the lull, the sailors on the *O'Bannon* raced aft toward the K-guns and managed to pull the cord to launch the depth charges mounted on top of the guns.

Arcing through the air, they landed in the water alongside the submarine. As they sank below the surface, they detonated directly under the sub, sending her to the bottom.

In recognition of this event, a few years later the Maine Potato Growers Association presented a plaque to the *O'Bannon* for using the lowly spud to sink a Japanese submarine. The plaque was mounted in the midships passage next to the spud locker

Chapter 9

A Game of Chicken

During the 1950s, with the Cold War in full swing, there was a race to see whether the Western nations or the Communist nations would dominate the world. Led by the United States, the forces of freedom were put to the test. Everywhere, from Africa to Central America, the Mideast, and Southeast Asia, even into outer space the communists were on the move.

One other area that was fiercely contested was the polar regions of the Arctic and Antarctic. To counter the threat, the Navy launched project SCMAP to map the vast reaches of the Arctic Ocean. Meanwhile, at the opposite end of the globe, Operation Deep Freeze got under way following a decision to establish a permanent base at McMurdo Sound, Antarctica.

To support this mission, Task Force 43, under the command of Admiral Dufek, was formed. The

USS Wyandot, an amphibious cargo ship from the World War II era, under the command of Captain Ronald K. Irving, was one of the ships assigned to this force.

In October 1955 the *Wyandot* steamed into Narragansett Bay to load supplies for MCB (Seabee) Battalion 21 at Davisville, Rhode Island. After she completed loading supplies she stopped briefly in Norfolk before she set sail for Antarctica on November 14.

Transiting the Panama Canal, the *Wyandot* set course for Auckland, New Zealand, the jumping-off point for Antarctica. With the vessel steaming independently, the long voyage to Auckland could best be described as one from nauseum to tedium as Thomas Heggen put it in his classic novel, *Mister Roberts*. The days at sea passed slowly by. Since they were well outside the shipping lanes, there weren't even any ship sightings to relieve the monotony.

About ten days out of the Panama Canal, the quiet on the bridge of the *Wyandot* was suddenly interrupted when the starboard lookout shouted out excitedly, "Ship ahoy!"

"Where away?" the officer of the deck replied.

"Dead ahead," the lookout answered.

Rushing out onto the wing of the bridge, the OOD swung the bearing circle around on the pelorus and took a bearing on the contact. A few minutes later he took another bearing. The bearing had not changed, which indicated to him that they were on a collision course. *Only two ships in this whole damn ocean, and we are headed straight for each other*, the OOD mused. *Must be something to the theory of magnetic attraction.*

Calling out for the messenger of the watch, he directed, "Notify the captain that we have a ship dead ahead at about 10 miles. She appears to be on a collision course."

With that, the messenger scurried off, headed for the captain's cabin. When he returned to the bridge a few moments later, the OOD asked, "What did the captain have to say?"

"He didn't say anything, sir."

As the two ships continued to close, the OOD closely monitored the bearing. It remained steady. When the range reached five miles, he again called for the messenger.

"Notify the captain that the contact has closed to five miles and still remains on a collision course. Request his permission to alter course to starboard and pass port to port." This would be in accordance with standard procedure as required under the International Rules of the Road.

Again the messenger went off to notify the captain. When he returned, the OOD asked, "What did he say?"

"Sir, the captain said that you are to maintain course and speed."

The OOD looked at him quizzically, "Are you sure that's what he said?"

"Yes, sir. I'm positive."

Although the captain was known to be a bit eccentric, this didn't make any sense.

The OOD continued to nervously take bearings, hoping to see some drift either to the right or left, but the bearing remained constant. The two ships had now closed to about three miles, close enough to distinctly make out the other vessel. She appeared to be a tramp steamer.

"Messenger, notify the captain that the range has now closed to three miles. The bearing remains constant. Request permission to alter course to starboard....and hurry."

Returning to the bridge out of breath, the messenger blurted out, "Sir, the captain says for you to maintain course and speed."

By now the other members of the bridge watch began to pay attention to what was happening. Ahead, the tramp steamer was now clearly visible through the bridge's portholes, and she was clearly headed straight for the *Wyandot*.

It was even more worrisome considering that she was a tramp steamer, as such vessels were notorious for being pretty relaxed when it came to maintaining lookouts and an alert bridge watch. More than likely the officer on watch was asleep somewhere.

The range had now closed to two miles. The bridge of the steamer was now clearly visible. There was no sign of activity.

"Messenger, tell the captain we are approaching extremis," the OOD ordered. "Urgently request his presence on the bridge."

The messenger rushed off to deliver the message. The range had now closed to one mile. The OOD was becoming desperate. *Should he take it upon himself to alter course against the captain's orders, or should he continue on toward certain disaster?*

"Captain on the bridge," the boatswain's mate called out. The OOD breathed a sigh of relief. At least now if there were to be a collision it would not be his fault.

"Request permission to alter course, Captain," the OOD asked again.

"Negative, maintain your heading," came the reply.

The range had now closed to under 1000 yards. Among the bridge watch there were numerous worried looks. Although all had wished for a little excitement, this was more than they wanted.

The eyes that weren't on the 'old man', wondering what he was going to do, were on the bridge of the steamer looming ever larger ahead.

The ships, by now, had closed to 500 yards. The OOD looked at the captain, anxiously awaiting orders. Captain Irving calmly took a seat in his chair on the port wing of the bridge, where he watched events unfold. Collision now appeared to be inevitable.

Suddenly there was a flurry of activity on the bridge of the steamer. Someone had finally awakened to realize what was happening. The bow of the steamer began to swing to starboard. The OOD closed his eyes. He couldn't bear to watch. He braced himself for the crash that he now felt was inevitable.

When it didn't happen, he opened his eyes to see the steamer passing down the port side almost close enough to shake hands. On its bridge, the captain looked to be frightened out of his wits. As the bridges passed each other, Captain Irving took off his hat and shouted over at the other skipper, "**Chicken.**"

After the ships had passed and the steamer receded toward the horizon, Captain Irving got out of his chair. "I am going below," he said calmly.

For at least this one day, the boredom of a long ocean passage had been lifted.

Chapter 10

The Big Boat Race

It was November 1952. The Korean War was in full swing. Four destroyers from CORTDESRON 21 (escort destroyer squadron 21) had just completed a six-month deployment to Westpac (Western Pacific), where they had been operating as part of Task Force 77 and 95 in the Sea of Japan and the Yellow Sea. Arriving at Midway Island, they put into port to take on fuel.

While there, the division commodore, Commander Blouin, called a meeting of his commanding officers. When they had all gathered in the wardroom, the commodore briefed them on the reason for the meeting.

"What do you think of the idea of having a race to Pearl?" he asked. "We all have to complete a full power run anyway. This will not only fulfill this requirement, it will also get us back home to Pearl a couple of days sooner."

There was an enthusiastic "let's do it" from all four skippers present.

"Okay then, we need to come up with a few ground rules," Blouin said.

After some discussion, it was agreed on to keep it simple. The four destroyers would line up abreast outside the entrance to the Midway channel. The skippers also agreed that each of the ships could have all four boilers on line, but they could not light off their super-heaters until after the signal starting the race. The finish line would be a line drawn 180 degrees true from Barbers Point Lighthouse on the island of Oahu.

"I guess that about does it," Blouin said.

After the meeting ended, the four skippers returned to their ships and called a meeting with their respective officers to plan their strategy. Of course, individual ship's speed would be an important factor, but fuel management would perhaps even be more important. Even under normal conditions, destroyers were renowned for being fuel guzzlers, but with all four boilers and super-heaters on line they could really eat up fuel.

Onboard the *Renshaw,* Captain Fulghum went over strategy with his operations officer, navigator, and engineering officer. From a navigation point of view, the operation was simple, plotting a rhumb line from Midway to the westernmost point of the island of Oahu. Fuel, however, was another matter. The engineering officer did some quick calculations. "It's going to be close, he said.

"What can we do to improve our odds?" Fulghum asked.

"One thing we could do is avoid taking on ballast," the engineering officer replied. Standard operating procedure called for replacing the fuel oil in the tanks with sea water as it was used up.

"What's the weather forecast?" the skipper asked, turning to his operations officer.

"Typically trade wind weather, Captain. Winds out of the northeast at 15 to 25 knots."

"Okay, we'll dispense with taking on ballast," the skipper replied. "Also, let's make sure our tanks are topped off. The last thing we want to do is run out of fuel and have to be towed into port.

"Anything else?" he asked.

"We need to get our best helmsman on the wheel," the ops officer replied. "Each time the rudder moves off of amidships it will slow us down. We need individuals who can keep the ship on course using as little rudder as possible."

"Okay, do it," Fulghum replied. "What else?"

"We could shut down the evaps. That will save some steam," the engineering officer said. "Our tanks are topped off. We should have enough fresh water to get us to Pearl."

"Make it so," Fulghum replied.

At 1500 the four destroyers sortied out of the channel from Midway and on signal lined up in a line abreast on a bearing of 225 degrees true, awaiting the signal from the commodore to start the race. Soon, the signalman called out, "Flag signal at the dip, Captain. It reads; *let the fun begin.*"

A moment later the signalman called out, "Signal close up." Then, "Execute."

The race had begun.

"All engines ahead flank. Make turns for maximum speed," the captain ordered. "Tell the engine room to light off super-heaters on all four boilers."

Super-heaters were a means of raising the ambient temperature of the steam from 212 degrees to 600 degrees Fahrenheit, thereby increasing the energy produced.

The stern dropped as the twin propellers bit into the water. Compared to other ships, a destroyer was more akin to an Indy car than to a family sedan. The ship leaped forward as the screws built up speed. Black smoke poured from the stacks of the four ships as the boilermen on watch attempted to regulate the air mixture.

On the bridge all eyes were on the knotmeter. Five, ten, fifteen, twenty, twenty-five, thirty, thirty-five, knots. By now the ship was shaking from stem to stern. Thirty-six, thirty-seven. The knotmeter now climbed more slowly.

"Ask the engine room if we can squeeze a little more out of her," the captain said.

A few seconds later the chief engineer's voice came over the 21 MC.

"We're pretty well wide open, Captain. We're in the process of making a few minor adjustments. I think after that we'll be able to get a few more turns out of her."

"Good," Fulghum replied. "Do the best you can."

As the ship raced along, the skipper settled into his chair on the wing of the bridge. It promised to be a long, uncomfortable night. Fortunately, the sea state was slight, making the ride more tolerable. While he sat there he mused over why the commodore had come up with having a race to Pearl Harbor. Obviously, it was intended to be a morale booster, but he suspected there were other motives as well. He figured that the commodore was looking to evaluate his skippers and see who would come up with the most ingenious ways to get the most out of their individual ships and crews.

"Thirty-seven knots, Captain," the OOD reported.

"Good," Fulghum replied.

As the hours passed, the knotmeter climbed slowly until it topped 39 knots. Off to port, the *Epperson* started to fall behind. This was not unexpected, as she was a Gearing class destroyer. Although newer, they were not as fast as the lighter, sleeker Fletcher class destroyers.

Around midnight, the *Phillips* reported a problem with her number three boiler and was dropping out of the race. This left only the *Nicholas* and the *Renshaw* still in the race.

As dawn broke, the two destroyers were still pretty much neck and neck.

Now if only the fuel holds out, Fulghum mused. Calling for the OOD, he said, "Get hold of the chief engineer and ask him to report to the bridge."

A few moments later the chief engineer appeared on the bridge. "You wanted to see me, Captain?"

"I was wondering how we are doing on fuel," the skipper replied.

"It's going to be touch and go. We have leaned out the mixture as far as we can and still maintain this speed."

"Okay, but if we have to lose a little speed to conserve fuel, let's do it, and please keep me advised."

"I should have a better idea in a couple of hours. It is difficult sounding the tanks while we are moving around like this."

Time wore on. "Ninety miles to the finish line, Captain," the navigator reported.

Now if only the fuel holds out, the skipper mused out loud. His thoughts were interrupted by the 21 MC. It was the chief engineer.

"How are we doing?" the captain asked.

"It's difficult getting a sounding on the tanks, but according to my calculations I think we will make it."

"Okay, do the best you can. We have less than ninety miles to go," the skipper replied.

Time passed by slowly. In the east the sky brightened as the sun raced westward toward the horizon.

"Forty miles to go," the navigator called out.

One more hour, the captain said to himself. Looking out on the port beam, he could see the *Nicholas* racing alongside.

For a few moments he dozed off in his chair. He was awakened by the voice of the OOD. "The *Nicholas* is falling back, captain. It looks like she has lost power."

A few seconds later the PriTac radio blared out, "This is 'Sandals', I am about to run out of fuel. I am dropping out of the race."

"How far to the finish line?" Fulghum asked.

"Twelve miles, Captain," the navigator replied.

Sitting in his chair, Fulghum watched the island of Oahu come into view to the east. He began to nod off.

Several minutes later, he was jarred awake by the voice of the navigator. "Barbers Point bearing 000 degrees. "Captain, we have won. We have won the race."

Hearing the news, a loud cheer arose from the bridge team. Now the crew would have something to brag about, after the embarrassing incident alongside the pier in Pearl Harbor several months ago.

"Tell the engine room to reduce speed and take the super-heaters off line," Fulghum said. "Also hoist a broom (signifying a clean sweep) from the yardarm."

About an hour and a half later, the *Renshaw,* her superstructure and stacks still riddled with shrapnel holes from a duel with an enemy shore battery in the vicinity of Ch'angjin, North Korea, rounded hospital point, and passed the Pearl Harbor Shipyard to starboard.

In the distance the sound of boatswain's pipes could be heard piping the various ships crews to morning colors.

Passing the Officers Club, Pier 1 came into view ahead where a large group of wives and girlfriends anxiously waited to welcome their hero's home from war.

Chapter 11

The Saga of the Willie Dee

Of all the sea stories there are probably none told as often as the saga of the destroyer, the USS *William D. Porter DD 579,* often called the "Willie Dee".
A Fletcher Class, 2100-ton destroyer, the *Porter* was named after a civil war admiral, William D. Porter. She was commissioned on 6 July, 1943 in Orange, Texas, with Lieutenant Commander Wilford A. Walter as commanding officer.

This much of the story is factual. From this point on the details vary somewhat, as is to be expected. The essential facts, however, remain the same.

After shaking down at Guantanamo Bay, Cuba the *Porter* arrived at her homeport at Norfolk, Virginia. For the next several weeks she conducted operations in and out of Norfolk with various units of the Atlantic Fleet.

In early November the *Porter* received orders to rendezvous off of Cape Henry, Virginia with the *USS Iowa*. Perhaps portending events to come, as the *Porter* backed out of her slip at the naval base, her port anchor raked the destroyer berthed astern, tearing down her lifelines and life rafts. With a quick apology from the skipper, she continued on her way around Sewell's Point and down the Thimble Shoals Channel to her rendezvous with the *Iowa*.

Although those onboard the *Porter* were unaware of it at the time, the *Iowa* had just picked up President Franklin D. Roosevelt from the presidential yacht *Potomac*, near the entrance to Chesapeake Bay to take him to Casablanca where the President and his entourage would fly to Cairo, Egypt to meet with Winston Churchill and then on to Teheran, Iran where they would meet with Joseph Stalin.

The *Porter*, along with several other destroyers, was to act as a screen to protect the *Iowa* from any German submarines that might be lurking underneath the sea en route to their destination.

Things quickly fell into a routine until, on the third day out, there was a large explosion between the screen and the *Iowa*. All ships went to general quarters, fearing a submarine attack. The cause of the explosion, as it turned out, was that the Willie Dee had accidentally rolled a depth charge off the stern. Unfortunately, it had not been set on safe, as it should have been.

For the next several days everything was pretty much routine. Admiral Ernest J. King, the chief of naval operations, was traveling with the President. Seeking to impress Roosevelt with the Navy's capability, he decided to have the destroyers run simulated torpedo attacks on the *Iowa*.

Eager to overcome the previous embarrassment resulting from the dropping of a depth charge, Captain Walter anxiously awaited his turn to make a run on the *Iowa*. When the time arrived, he ordered, "All ahead flank speed, right full rudder. Come to course 175 degrees."

The ship heeled sharply to port as the single rudder sped the ship into her turn. Heading directly for the *Iowa's* beam, he waited for the range to close to 4000 yards before ordering, "Left full rudder, come to course 270." This would put him on a parallel course to the *Iowa* and free his midship torpedo launcher.

When the helmsman reported "Steady on course 270," the skipper gave the order, "Torpedo control, simulate launching a full spread of torpedoes. I say again, Simulate. Do not launch."

A few seconds later there was a loud *whoosh*. Looking aft, the captain watched in horror as a live torpedo left the tube and headed straight for the *Iowa* at forty knots. Even though radio silence was in effect, he nevertheless grabbed the radio handset and called the *Iowa* to notify her that a live torpedo was under way and urging her to take evasive action.

Receiving the transmission, the OOD on the *Iowa* ordered right full rudder to present a bow aspect to the oncoming torpedo, thereby reducing chances of a hit.

The *Iowa* spun sharply to starboard. Roosevelt wondered what the devil was going on. When he was informed that a live torpedo had been accidentally launched in their direction, he reportedly ordered that his wheelchair be wheeled closer to the rail so he could watch.

Fortunately, the torpedo missed, and exploded in the *Iowa's* wake 3000 yards astern.

Admiral King was furious. He demanded to know who was responsible. When the skipper of the Willie Dee, meekly admitted, "We did it," Admiral King ordered the *Porter* detached from the force with orders to proceed to the naval station in Bermuda for a formal investigation as to what had happened.

When the Willie Dee arrived in Bermuda, a squad of Marines blocked the gangway and placed the entire crew under arrest. It is reportedly the only time in the annals of the U. S. Navy that an entire ship's company was placed under arrest.

The investigation revealed that a torpedoman named Dawson had accidentally left a live primer in one of the tubes. Later, when he found the spent primer, he threw it over the side to hide the evidence. He was given a court-martial and sentenced to fifteen years in prison. The sentence was later commuted by President Roosevelt.

When the crew was finally allowed to go ashore in Bermuda, they were greeted in the various clubs and bars on the island with shouts of "Don't shoot. We're Republicans."

Whether it was punishment or operational considerations, the Willie Dee was next ordered to duty in the Aleutian Islands. Transiting the Panama Canal, she briefly stopped in San Diego to pick up cold-weather gear and other supplies before heading for the North Pacific.

Arriving at Dutch Harbor, Alaska she conducted training operations as part of Task Force 94. After a brief stint escorting a destroyer tender, *Blackhawk,* from Hawaii to Adak in the Aleutians, she resumed operations out of Dutch Harbor, escorting ships along the Aleutian chain.

On one occasion, while tied up at the pier at Dutch Harbor, the old nemesis struck again. Whatever his reason, whether accidental or deliberate, one of the gunners mates loaded a live five- inch shell in mount 51 and then proceeded to fire it off. As bad luck would have it, the errant projectile landed in the front yard of the base commander, who was having a party at the time. Luckily, no one was hurt.

The Willie Dee was off again, this time for a brief period in the shipyard at Mare Island, California before heading off for the Philippines, arriving just in time for the Battle of Leyte Gulf. From this point on the luck of the *Porter* changed, and she managed to shoot down several Japanese planes, along with conducting shore bombardment in support of the ongoing amphibious operation.

Following the Battle of Leyte Gulf, the Willie Dee was ordered to Okinawa in support of the amphibious operation about to begin there.

As the battle for the island went on, the Japanese became desperate, launching kamikaze suicide, attacks against the main U.S. force supporting the landing.

The Willie Dee was on radar picket, or tomcat duty as it was called in Navy circles. Positioned between the main force and the Japanese island of Kyushu, from which many of the kamikaze raids were launched, the ship brought down an additional five enemy planes.

Her run of good luck was not to hold, however.

At 0815 on the morning of 10 June, 1945, an Achii D3A Val dive bomber dropped below the clouds and made straight for the Willie Dee. Although the ship managed to evade the suicide bomber and shoot it down, the plane ended up directly under the ship, where it exploded. The ship's back was broken. Although the crew struggled valiantly for three hours to keep the ship afloat, it was to no avail. The skipper gave the order to abandon ship, and twelve minutes later the ship heeled over to starboard and disappeared beneath the waves.

Miraculously, there were no fatalities, largely because of the efforts of Lieutenant Richard McCool, the commanding officer of an LCS (amphibious landing ship) that happened to be in the vicinity.

For his heroism, McCool was awarded the Medal of Honor, and the Willie Dee passed into Navy History.

Chapter 12

The Homecoming

In all the lexicons of naval warfare, none is perhaps as complex as that of amphibious warfare. Not only does it require the utmost in coordination and planning, it also requires special types of ships to deliver in a timely fashion the large amounts of rolling stock, tanks, trucks, etc, required to support the landing force ashore.

To help meet these special requirements the LST was conceived. Mobilizing shipyards throughout the United States, over 800 of this type of ship were built between 1942 and 1945. Considered expendable, they were not even named, just assigned a number. Underpowered, with their squared off bow, high sides and flat bottom, they were notorious for rolling and pounding in any kind of heavy sea.

Although not ranking very high in the pecking order of Navy combatant ships, they nevertheless required a high degree of seamanship skills to operate.

For all other types of ships, going aground was something to be avoided at all costs. For the LST, however, going aground, safely unloading her cargo and getting off the beach was her only mission. To do so successfully, required taking into account many factors, including long-shore currents, beach gradients, sea state and offshore sand bars etc.

LST 325 was launched on 27 October, 1942 and commissioned at the Philadelphia Navy Shipyard on 1 February, 1943. After completing shakedown, she chopped to COMPHIBLANT (commander amphibious command Atlantic Fleet) for duty. Shortly thereafter, she received orders to get under way for the Mediterranean. After a brief stopover in Bermuda, she arrived in Oran, Algeria in April. During the next three months, she practiced landing exercises along the coast of North Africa before participating in the landings at Gela, Sicily, and Salerno, Italy.

In November of 1943, she joined the mass of ships being assembled in England in preparation for the invasion of Normandy. On D-Day plus 2, she anchored off Omaha Beach where she successfully discharged her cargo of 59 vehicles, 13 officers, and 408 enlisted men. On her return she carried 43 casualties back to England. In the ensuing days and weeks she made over 40 trips across the channel, ferrying thousands of troops and untold quantities of vehicles and heavy equipment to the battle zone.

In May 1945, with the war in Europe winding down, the *LST-325* returned to the States where she underwent voyage repairs and a refit. Just before she was due to leave for the Pacific Theater, the war with Japan ended.

In July 1946 she was decommissioned and placed in the reserve fleet at Green Cove Springs, Florida. She remained there until 1951 when she was transferred to the Military Sea Transportation Service (MSTS). For the next ten years she operated in support of the construction of the DEW (Defense Early Warning) Line being built across Canada. 1961 she was decommissioned once more and returned to the reserve fleet. Then in 1964 she was reactivated and transferred to Greece as part of a grant-in-aid package.

End of story....not quite. In 2000 the Greek government announced that the aging LST was going to be sold for scrap. Upon hearing this sad news, a group of retired "gator" (amphibious) sailors got together and decided to do something about it.

They approached the Greek government with a request that the ship be turned over to them instead. The Greek government agreed to do so, providing the ship was picked up in Crete where she now lay.

The group was now faced with the task of assembling a crew of all the required specialties to make the ship seaworthy and then sail her back to the States. Obtaining volunteers proved to be quite easy, although many of those who volunteered were now in their sixties and even seventies.

Since there was no money available, the volunteer crew had to pay their way to Crete and 'cumshaw' (beg, borrow or midnight requisition) the material they would need to make the necessary repairs. They also had to find a city that would sponsor them if they were successful in getting the ship back to the States.

Inquiries to Jacksonville, Florida and Norfolk, Virginia were met with little enthusiasm. The skipper noticed on the internet that Mobile, Alabama had a collection of museum ships. He put in a call to the military coordinator in the city government who luckily happened to be a retired navy captain. After listening to what the skipper had to say, he promised to bring it up with the city fathers who agreed to sponsor the ship if the crew could get her back to the States. *This was a big if.*

While this was going on, work on the LST continued. Getting the engines and generators working were obviously the highest priority. Time passed as the crew worked feverishly to get the engines working. Finally, both engines and one generator were back in operation.

Getting a load of fuel to take them back to the States was the next task. The approached British Petroleum who generously agreed to provide 16,000 gallons of diesel. The hitch was that the fuel had to be picked up in Piraeus, Greece, some 150 miles away.

But, that wasn't the only problem. The port director in Crete had declared the ship unsafe to put to sea. After much cajoling, the captain convinced the port director to allow him to put to sea at least for one day in order to conduct sea trials.

Arriving at the sea buoy outside the harbor, the skipper ordered that course be set for Piraeus. The port director decided it was futile to protest. Besides, he was glad to get the 'rust bucket' out of his harbor anyway.

After picking up the load of fuel in Piraeus, the *LST-325* got underway and set course for its next port of call, Gibraltar. While en route the only working generator began to act up. Limping into Gibraltar, the wayward LST tied up at the British Dockyard. Sympathetic to their plight, the supervisor of the dockyard donated a rebuilt generator to replace the ailing one.

By now, the news organizations began to take note and carry the story. With the story becoming national news, the U.S. Coast Guard decided to get into the act. U. S. Coast Guard inspectors paid a visit to the ship in Gibraltar and declared it unsafe to make a transAtlantic crossing. The crew told the Coast Guard to stick it and put to sea anyway.

Fortunately, the weather remained good and the crossing was uneventful. After a brief layover in the Bahamas to make some voyage repairs, the ship finally arrived in Mobile to a tumultuous welcome.

Following a period in dry dock to take care of the bottom, the *LST-325* made several goodwill tours up and down the east coast of the United States, before finding a permanent home in Evansville, Indiana. It is fitting that her final resting place lay along the Ohio River where so many of her sister ships were built.

All this happened because a group of retired *gators* refused to allow their beloved ship be cut up for scrap.